For Bruce for taking
me into the blue – FM
To my daughter Kai – AB

First published in the United Kingdom in 2004 by Ragged Bears Publishing Limited,
Milborne Wick, Sherborne, Dorset DT9 4PW
www.raggedbears.co.uk

Distributed by Ragged Bears Limited, Nightingale House, England's Lane,
Queen Camel, Somerset BA22 7NN Tel: 01935 851590

HB ISBN 1 85714 270 5
PB ISBN 1 85714 271 3

Printed in China

Into The Blue

Written by Frances McKay

Illustrated by Andrew Breakspeare

RAGGED BEARS

Milborne Wick, Dorset • Brooklyn, New York

One morning, Ursula found an
envelope on the mat.
It said: *To Miss Ursula.*
'That's me,' she said and opened it.

To Miss Ursula

Inside was a blue paper circle.
'What is it Oscar?' asked Ursula.
'Hush . . .' said Oscar. 'You'll find out later!'

That night, Ursula took the blue circle
and put it on the table next to her bed.
It started to glow and change colour.

When Ursula tried to pick it up, it flew
out of her hands and across the room.
'Come on,' said Oscar, 'follow me!'

The paper circle had become a blue
hole and Oscar disappeared through it!
Without stopping to think, Ursula
jumped out of bed and followed him.

The hole led into a dark, dark tunnel.
When Ursula looked back, her bedroom
had vanished and the blue hole was
bouncing towards her like a ball.

She caught the ball and it started
to glow, brighter and brighter.
'Do come on Ursula,' said Oscar.
'It's this way.'

They came out of the tunnel and into a strange forest.
'Which way now?' said Ursula.
'It's this way,' said Oscar. 'No, wait a minute,
it's this way. Or perhaps it's this way?'

'Oscar, we're lost!' said Ursula.
'Of course we're not!' said Oscar.

At that moment, the blue light started to
glow again and jumped out of Ursula's hand.

Ursula gasped as the ball landed on the ground and opened out into a round hole in the forest floor.

'Come on Ursula, it's definitely
this way!' said Oscar.

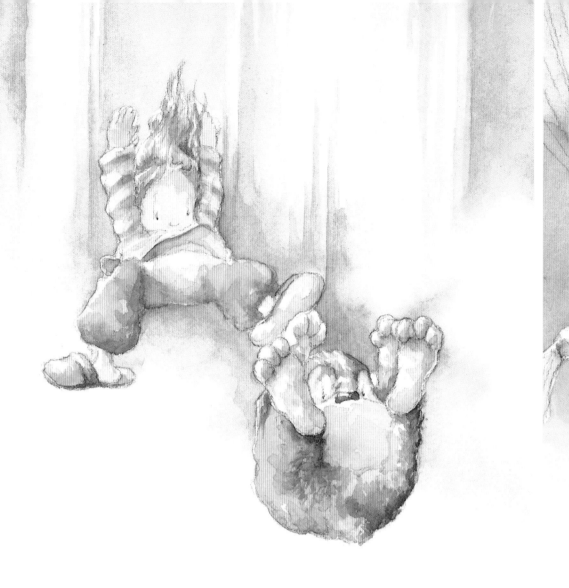

Ursula followed Oscar and
jumped through the hole.
Down and down they fell,
tumbling over and over.
'I'm not sure I'm enjoying
this Oscar,' said Ursula.

But when Ursula
looked up, the hole
had opened out
into a beautiful
blue parachute
and she and Oscar
were floating
gently downwards.

Ursula could see the sea stretching
out in all directions below them.
'Oh dear,' she said, 'I can't swim.'
'Don't worry,' said Oscar, 'neither can I.'

But instead of dropping into the deep blue sea, they landed with a bump in a small boat. And the parachute turned into a huge blue sail.

It filled with wind
and pulled them along.
'I'm good at this,'
said Oscar, 'I'll steer.'

The boat leapt
off a big rolling
wave and floated
up into the sky.

'I didn't know boats
could fly,' said Oscar.

Ursula looked down. She could see land, a town, houses and gardens and then there was her house . . .and it was getting closer and closer.

Before Ursula knew what had happened, they were bouncing on her bed. And the blue sail flattened out and became her bedroom ceiling.

'Well,' said Ursula, 'I wonder who sent me that?'
'I know,' said Oscar, 'but it's a secret.'
'It was you, wasn't it Oscar!' said Ursula.
'I can't wait to see what comes in the post tomorrow!'